THIS JOURNAL BELONGS TO

How to use this journal

This journal is all about documenting your travels to Yellowstone and The Grand Tetons National Parks. The journal is broken up into a few sections.

1) A place to write down your packing list, park maps, and an area to record what you want to do when you get there.

2) Enough pages to document 12 travel days. Two pages for each day. If you are on a longer trip you can use one page for each day.

3) Blank pages. See below for fun ideas you can try on those pages.

4) Activity pages with coloring, word searches, mazes, and more!

5) Information about animals and a place to mark which animals you saw.

6) Challenge questions about your trip. Feel free to include photos or drawings!

7) A few blank note pages for you to write any thoughts about your trip or ideas for next time.

IDEAS FOR THE BLANK PAGES

- Photos, drawings, doodles, notes, or journal entries.
- Tickets (Airplane, bus, tour receipts, etc.)
- Maps
- Trip itinerary
- Park brochures
- Postcards
- Draw the most interesting/unique thing you saw
- Places to visit, see, or eat at next time you go there
- An item you wished you had packed
- A quote you saw on your trip
- The name of someone you met
- A cool bookmark
- A pressed coin
- An etching of a stone, raised street name, or a texture
- Stickers
- Describe your hotel or campsite
- What was your first thought when you arrived?

ACTIVITY IDEAS

Young or old, activities can make the time you spend in our beautiful national parks more interesting, educational, and fun. Here are a few ideas to try out.

- Stand with your back against the tallest tree you can find and look up. What do you see? Any birds, insects, or animals?

- Find a quiet area without crowds. Sit down, close your eyes and listen. What do you hear? Write down all the sounds. Move to a different location and do the same thing. Do you hear anything different? What's the same?

- Find an ant. Follow it to see where it is going or what it is doing.

- Find a bird. What does it look like? How does it sound? Take a picture.

- Look for wet ground or mud. Do you see any animal tracks?

- Close your eyes and try to listen for insects? Can you figure out where they are by sound? Try to look for them.

- Find flowers. Don't pick them but get down close and count the petals. Describe the color(s). Draw a picture or take a photo.

- Take a piece of string (or something else you can mark a small area off with) and make a ring around a small area. Take notes on what you find by drawing a picture of everything in the area or just describing it.

- Find a beautiful rock and create a story about how it got there.

- With a magnifying glass check out an insect, leave, flower, or rock. What details did you miss when you looked with just your eyes?

- Take a hike and pay close attention to the sounds and smells around you. Often, we only look with our eyes, but using your other senses can help you experience more of the nature around you.

- Close your eyes. Can you feel a breeze? Is it warm or cool?

ADULTS (and kids too) take a moment to close your eyes, take a deep breath, and enjoy the natural beauty around you.

NOTE: Remember to not pick leaves or flowers and leave rocks or other items just where you found them so others can enjoy the park.

Packing Lists

Day time clothes

- [ ]
- [ ]
- [ ]
- [ ]
- [ ]
- [ ]
- [ ]

Evening clothes

- [ ]
- [ ]
- [ ]
- [ ]
- [ ]
- [ ]
- [ ]

Underwear etc

- [ ]
- [ ]
- [ ]
- [ ]
- [ ]
- [ ]
- [ ]

Extras

- [ ]
- [ ]
- [ ]
- [ ]
- [ ]
- [ ]
- [ ]

Packing Lists

BackPack
- ☐
- ☐
- ☐
- ☐
- ☐
- ☐
- ☐

Essentials
- ☐
- ☐
- ☐
- ☐
- ☐
- ☐
- ☐

Toiletries
- ☐
- ☐
- ☐
- ☐
- ☐
- ☐
- ☐

Electronics
- ☐
- ☐
- ☐
- ☐
- ☐
- ☐
- ☐

Yellowstone Map

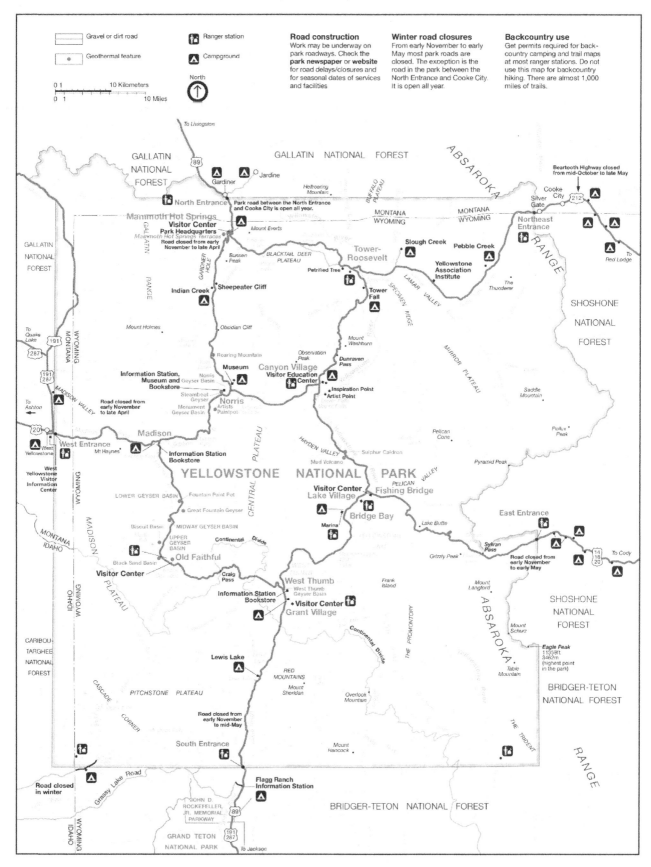

Yellowstone map is a public domain image provided by NPS.
Meant for general reference and NOT for backcountry exploration.

Yellowstone Bucket List

PLACES I WANT TO VISIT:

THINGS I WANT TO SEE:

TOP 3 DESTINATIONS:

Grand Tetons Map

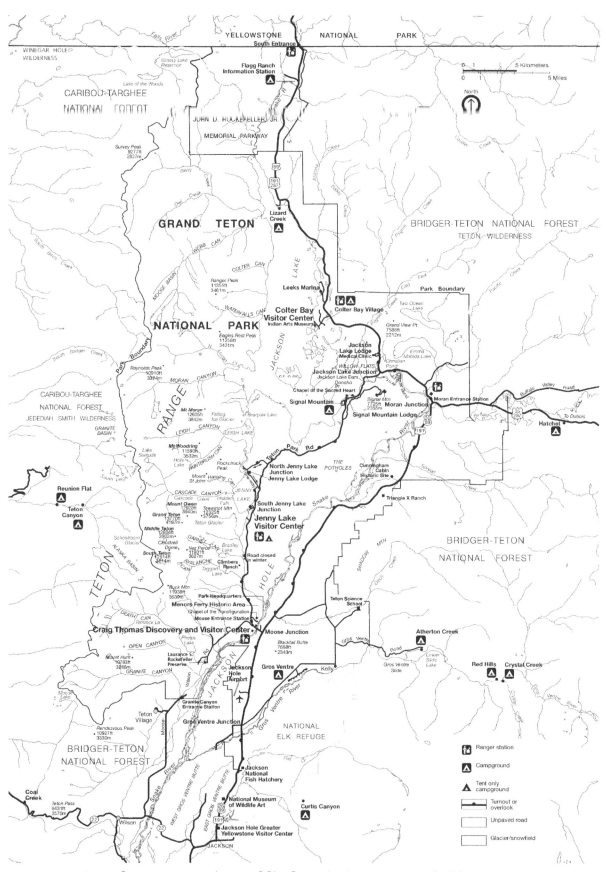

Grand Tetons map is a public domain image provided by NPS.
Meant for general reference and NOT for backcountry exploration.

Grand Teton Bucket List

PLACES I WANT TO VISIT:

THINGS I WANT TO SEE:

TOP 3 DESTINATIONS:

I AM IN _____

THREE THINGS I SAW TODAY

TODAY I ATE _____

AND IT TASTED   GREAT   AWESOME   HEAVENLY
                HORRIBLE   TERRIBLE   OKAY

WHO CAME WITH ME

IF I WENT HERE AGAIN I WOULD

DRAW AN EMOJI TO
DESCRIBE THE DAY

I GIVE THIS TRIP ☆☆☆☆

TODAY WAS

AWESOME   FUN   COOL   TERRIFIC
OKAY   BORING   EXHAUSTING

TODAY'S DATE

I AM IN
_____

BEST PART OF MY DAY
_____
_____
_____

WORST PART OF MY DAY
_____
_____
_____

WEATHER REPORT

TRAVEL
DOODLE

TWO THINGS I LEARNED

_____
_____
_____
_____
_____
_____
_____

I AM IN _____

THREE THINGS I SAW TODAY

TODAY I ATE _____

AND IT TASTED
GREAT   AWESOME   HEAVENLY
HORRIBLE   TERRIBLE   OKAY

WHO CAME WITH ME

_____
_____
_____
_____
_____
_____

IF I WENT HERE AGAIN I WOULD

_____
_____
_____
_____
_____
_____

DRAW AN EMOJI TO
DESCRIBE THE DAY

I GIVE THIS TRIP ☆☆☆☆

TODAY WAS   AWESOME FUN COOL TERRIFIC
            OKAY   BORING   EXHAUSTING

TODAY'S DATE

I AM IN
_____

BEST PART OF MY DAY
_____
_____
_____

WORST PART OF MY DAY
_____
_____
_____

WEATHER REPORT

TRAVEL
DOODLE

TWO THINGS I LEARNED

_____
_____
_____
_____
_____
_____
_____

I AM IN _____

THREE THINGS I SAW TODAY

WHO CAME WITH ME

TODAY I ATE _____

AND IT TASTED GREAT   AWESOME   HEAVENLY
               HORRIBLE   TERRIBLE   OKAY

_____
_____
_____
_____
_____

IF I WENT HERE AGAIN I WOULD

_____
_____
_____
_____
_____
_____
_____
_____

DRAW AN EMOJI TO
DESCRIBE THE DAY

I GIVE THIS TRIP ☆☆☆☆

TODAY WAS   AWESOME   FUN   COOL   TERRIFIC
              OKAY   BORING   EXHAUSTING

TODAY'S DATE

I AM IN
_____

BEST PART OF MY DAY
_____
_____
_____
_____

WORST PART OF MY DAY
_____
_____
_____
_____

WEATHER REPORT

TRAVEL
DOODLE

TWO THINGS I LEARNED

_____
_____
_____
_____
_____
_____
_____

I AM IN _____

THREE THINGS I SAW TODAY

TODAY I ATE _____

AND IT TASTED   GREAT   AWESOME   HEAVENLY
                 HORRIBLE   TERRIBLE   OKAY

IF I WENT HERE AGAIN I WOULD

_____
_____
_____
_____
_____
_____
_____
_____

WHO CAME WITH ME

_____
_____
_____
_____
_____

DRAW AN EMOJI TO
DESCRIBE THE DAY

I GIVE THIS TRIP ☆ ☆ ☆ ☆

TODAY WAS

AWESOME   FUN   COOL   TERRIFIC
OKAY   BORING   EXHAUSTING

TODAY'S DATE

I AM IN
_____

BEST PART OF MY DAY
_____
_____
_____
_____

WORST PART OF MY DAY
_____
_____
_____
_____

WEATHER REPORT

TRAVEL DOODLE

TWO THINGS I LEARNED

_____
_____
_____
_____
_____
_____
_____
_____

I AM IN _____

THREE THINGS I SAW TODAY

WHO CAME WITH ME

TODAY I ATE _____

AND IT TASTED   GREAT   AWESOME   HEAVENLY
                 HORRIBLE   TERRIBLE   OKAY

IF I WENT HERE AGAIN I WOULD

_____
_____
_____
_____
_____
_____
_____
_____

_____
_____
_____
_____
_____
_____

DRAW AN EMOJI TO
DESCRIBE THE DAY

I GIVE THIS TRIP ☆☆☆☆

TODAY WAS

AWESOME   FUN   COOL   TERRIFIC
OKAY   BORING   EXHAUSTING

TODAY'S DATE

I AM IN
_____

BEST PART OF MY DAY
_____
_____
_____

WORST PART OF MY DAY
_____
_____
_____

WEATHER REPORT

TRAVEL
DOODLE

TWO THINGS I LEARNED

I AM IN _____

THREE THINGS I SAW TODAY

WHO CAME WITH ME

TODAY I ATE _____

AND IT TASTED   GREAT   AWESOME   HEAVENLY
                 HORRIBLE   TERRIBLE   OKAY

_____

_____

_____

_____

_____

IF I WENT HERE AGAIN I WOULD

_____

_____

_____

_____

_____

_____

_____

DRAW AN EMOJI TO
DESCRIBE THE DAY

I GIVE THIS TRIP ☆ ☆ ☆ ☆

TODAY WAS

AWESOME   FUN   COOL   TERRIFIC
OKAY   BORING   EXHAUSTING

TODAY'S DATE

I AM IN
_____

BEST PART OF MY DAY
_____
_____
_____
_____

WORST PART OF MY DAY
_____
_____
_____
_____

WEATHER REPORT

TRAVEL DOODLE

TWO THINGS I LEARNED

I AM IN _____

THREE THINGS I SAW TODAY

TODAY I ATE _____

AND IT TASTED   GREAT   AWESOME   HEAVENLY
                 HORRIBLE   TERRIBLE   OKAY

WHO CAME WITH ME

IF I WENT HERE AGAIN I WOULD

DRAW AN EMOJI TO
DESCRIBE THE DAY

I GIVE THIS TRIP

TODAY WAS

AWESOME FUN COOL TERRIFIC
OKAY BORING EXHAUSTING

TODAY'S DATE

I AM IN
_____

BEST PART OF MY DAY
_____
_____
_____

WORST PART OF MY DAY
_____
_____
_____
_____

WEATHER REPORT

TWO THINGS I LEARNED

TRAVEL
DOODLE

_____
_____
_____
_____
_____
_____

I AM IN _____

THREE THINGS I SAW TODAY

WHO CAME WITH ME

TODAY I ATE _____

AND IT TASTED   GREAT   AWESOME   HEAVENLY
                 HORRIBLE   TERRIBLE   OKAY

IF I WENT HERE AGAIN I WOULD

DRAW AN EMOJI TO
DESCRIBE THE DAY

I GIVE THIS TRIP ☆☆☆☆

TODAY WAS   AWESOME   FUN   COOL   TERRIFIC
             OKAY   BORING   EXHAUSTING

TODAY'S DATE

I AM IN
_____

BEST PART OF MY DAY
_____
_____
_____

WORST PART OF MY DAY
_____
_____
_____
_____

WEATHER REPORT

TRAVEL DOODLE

TWO THINGS I LEARNED

_____
_____
_____
_____
_____
_____
_____

I AM IN _____

THREE THINGS I SAW TODAY

TODAY I ATE _____

AND IT TASTED
GREAT   AWESOME   HEAVENLY
HORRIBLE   TERRIBLE   OKAY

WHO CAME WITH ME

_____
_____
_____
_____
_____

IF I WENT HERE AGAIN I WOULD

_____
_____
_____
_____
_____
_____
_____

DRAW AN EMOJI TO DESCRIBE THE DAY

I GIVE THIS TRIP ☆☆☆☆

TODAY WAS

TODAY'S DATE

I AM IN
_____

BEST PART OF MY DAY
_____
_____
_____
_____

WORST PART OF MY DAY
_____
_____
_____
_____

WEATHER REPORT

TRAVEL DOODLE

TWO THINGS I LEARNED

_____
_____
_____
_____
_____
_____
_____

I AM IN _____

THREE THINGS I SAW TODAY

TODAY I ATE _____

AND IT TASTED   GREAT   AWESOME   HEAVENLY
                HORRIBLE   TERRIBLE   OKAY

IF I WENT HERE AGAIN I WOULD

_____

_____

_____

_____

_____

_____

_____

WHO CAME WITH ME

_____

_____

_____

_____

_____

DRAW AN EMOJI TO
DESCRIBE THE DAY

I GIVE THIS TRIP

TODAY WAS

AWESOME FUN COOL TERRIFIC
OKAY BORING EXHAUSTING

TODAY'S DATE

I AM IN
_____

BEST PART OF MY DAY
_____
_____
_____
_____

WORST PART OF MY DAY
_____
_____
_____
_____

WEATHER REPORT

TRAVEL
DOODLE

TWO THINGS I LEARNED

_____
_____
_____
_____
_____
_____
_____

I AM IN _____

THREE THINGS I SAW TODAY

TODAY I ATE _____

AND IT TASTED   GREAT   AWESOME   HEAVENLY
                HORRIBLE   TERRIBLE   OKAY

WHO CAME WITH ME

IF I WENT HERE AGAIN I WOULD

DRAW AN EMOJI TO
DESCRIBE THE DAY

I GIVE THIS TRIP ☆☆☆☆

TODAY WAS

AWESOME FUN COOL TERRIFIC
OKAY BORING EXHAUSTING

TODAY'S DATE

I AM IN
_____

BEST PART OF MY DAY
_____
_____
_____

WORST PART OF MY DAY
_____
_____
_____

WEATHER REPORT

TWO THINGS I LEARNED

_____
_____
_____
_____
_____
_____
_____

TRAVEL DOODLE

I AM IN _____

THREE THINGS I SAW TODAY

TODAY I ATE _____

AND IT TASTED GREAT AWESOME HEAVENLY
HORRIBLE TERRIBLE OKAY

IF I WENT HERE AGAIN I WOULD
_____
_____
_____
_____
_____
_____
_____

WHO CAME WITH ME
_____
_____
_____
_____
_____

DRAW AN EMOJI TO
DESCRIBE THE DAY

I GIVE THIS TRIP ☆☆☆☆

TODAY WAS

AWESOME   FUN   COOL   TERRIFIC
OKAY   BORING   EXHAUSTING

TODAY'S DATE

I AM IN
_____

BEST PART OF MY DAY
_____
_____
_____
_____

WORST PART OF MY DAY
_____
_____
_____
_____

WEATHER REPORT

TWO THINGS I LEARNED

TRAVEL
DOODLE

 CAMP

 CAMP

 CAMP

 CAMP

 CAMP

 CAMP

 CAMP

Word Search

Warning the words can be up, down, diagonal, or backward.

```
A  P  Z  Q  P  B  C  P  U  U  U  U  F  A  W
W  M  G  T  D  E  S  J  G  V  G  A  Q  Q  A
M  O  O  Z  I  V  L  D  T  N  S  S  F  E  Q
M  U  X  Z  C  H  W  I  Q  S  Q  C  A  F  H
Z  N  Q  Y  D  H  B  C  C  B  A  Q  T  X  U
M  T  B  W  N  I  I  U  U  A  R  O  O  N  D
X  A  I  S  Y  F  S  C  L  N  N  V  Q  A  O
T  I  X  Y  G  O  O  S  K  U  U  F  C  V  T
O  N  T  E  J  B  N  R  P  A  L  D  D  F  Z
C  C  S  S  J  E  L  G  A  E  D  E  B  G  E
M  I  D  L  M  D  I  P  P  E  R  E  D  A  S
L  M  K  L  V  E  E  Z  V  L  B  R  E  U  F
G  A  I  O  T  G  K  B  Z  K  Z  U  R  U  Z
Y  T  G  P  W  G  B  F  J  A  W  C  M  W  A
F  K  A  E  N  O  T  S  W  O  L  L  E  Y  R
```

BEAR	DIPPER	PELICAN
BISON	EAGLE	YELLOWSTONE
CHICKADEE	ELK	
DEER	MOUNTAIN	

BEAR

Navigate the bear maze from start to end and color the picture

WORD SCRAMBLE

Unscramble the all the words below that have something to do with
Yellowstone or the Grand Tetons.

OCOEYT

_ _ _ _ _ _

RATOMM

_ _ _ _ _ _

YOERSP

_ _ _ _ _ _

AIPMSICRT

_ _ _ _ _ _ _ _ _

LITAR

_ _ _ _ _

RTCKSA

_ _ _ _ _ _

SNBIO

_ _ _ _ _

LGIZYZR

_ _ _ _ _ _ _

EHIK

_ _ _ _

Our Family Trip

Below is a story about your family trip. Ask one of your family members to give you words to fill out the blank spaces. Don't let them peek when you ask for words! Read the story out loud once all the spaces are filled.

Today was the _____ day of our entire trip! We woke up early and ate
descriptive word

the best _____ ever! I had ____ of them. My stomach was so full
a food   *number*

that I thought it would burst. Next, we went to _____.
place at the park

_____ was so amazed that he ran around screaming, "_____
name

_____!" It took me _____ to calm him down.
something you would yell   *a length of time*

Then, _____ decided we should take a hike. I had eaten so many
name

_____ that morning that I didn't want to hike. I suggested we
a food

go to _____ instead. When we got there, we saw _____ bison.
place at the park   *number*

People were getting really close to take _____. One person almost
plural noun

got gored by one of its _____. I stayed far enough away, but I still
a part of an animal

got a _____ picture.
descriptive word

The best part of the day was when _____ bought us ice cream! We
name

also got to go the visitor center and get something from the store. I

got _____. Today was the _____ day ever!
gift shop item   *descriptive word*

Bison

Navigate the bison maze from start to end and color the picture

WORD SEARCH

Warning the words can be up, down, diagonal, or backward.

```
U  R  E  V  T  E  B  P  N  J  W  E  S  H  C
B  E  P  R  C  Y  L  X  H  F  F  Q  X  H  M
T  C  J  W  O  L  D  F  A  I  T  H  F  U  L
K  J  B  Q  H  Y  W  A  X  L  J  R  V  T  X
C  I  N  A  C  L  O  V  Q  A  Q  N  A  Z  D
G  P  Y  K  J  I  N  D  C  V  X  X  B  I  A
S  O  U  P  A  T  T  Q  K  A  M  G  Q  K  L
U  D  S  M  R  N  Z  A  I  I  N  E  U  B  J
A  P  W  F  C  T  M  V  M  E  G  Y  D  U  B
G  Y  L  T  H  B  O  L  J  S  R  S  O  Y  L
H  A  G  L  J  R  U  F  B  I  I  E  V  N  I
T  J  U  Y  Z  I  T  F  O  D  C  R  V  E  W
O  L  J  N  T  O  P  D  U  M  R  S  P  I  W
N  J  I  W  D  M  X  H  E  S  U  L  F  U  R
Q  B  S  E  X  C  S  B  F  Y  R  U  Y  A  T
```

CANYON   OLDFAITHFUL   TRAIL

GEYSERS   PRISMATIC   VOLCANIC

LAVA   RIVER

MUDPOT   SULFUR

Color the mountains, lake, and sky every color you have seen today!

National Park Badges

Color the badges below and design a few of your own!

Geysers

Geysers send boiling hot water into the air. So, don't be like these silly tourists. Have fun finding all the things they are doing wrong. Add color to the page.

BALD EAGLE

Navigate the bald eagle maze from start to end and color the picture

WORD SEARCH

Warning the words can be up, down, diagonal, or backward.

```
K  D  K  Z  R  V  E  N  X  O  T  H  I  A  T
E  U  Y  I  D  U  Y  C  T  F  Z  K  L  P  J
N  K  E  C  B  P  T  N  T  N  P  E  F  N  T
P  F  I  S  H  Y  I  K  A  A  P  L  E  Y  A
I  Z  R  H  O  I  V  Z  H  A  M  Q  A  R  W
U  J  K  J  K  O  P  L  O  W  M  Y  L  E  W
G  O  K  C  C  W  M  M  W  G  J  G  R  O  Q
Z  X  I  L  E  R  R  I  U  Q  S  N  B  W  F
C  G  W  E  A  N  Z  O  Q  N  S  G  Q  Y  Q
N  O  T  E  T  W  J  S  J  X  K  I  O  E  Y
R  O  U  T  D  O  O  R  S  M  R  S  O  U  M
A  E  N  G  B  L  J  U  B  Z  D  T  L  T  F
N  B  I  U  A  F  V  I  H  Y  G  I  F  U  P
N  N  A  T  U  R  E  E  B  S  B  S  B  B  E
Z  W  U  V  G  D  B  Q  B  U  B  H  T  R  D
```

CHIPMUNK   MOOSE   TETON
COUGAR   NATURE   WOLF
FISH   OUTDOORS
HIKE   SQUIRREL

THE GRAND PRISMATIC

Color your own version of The Grand Prismatic

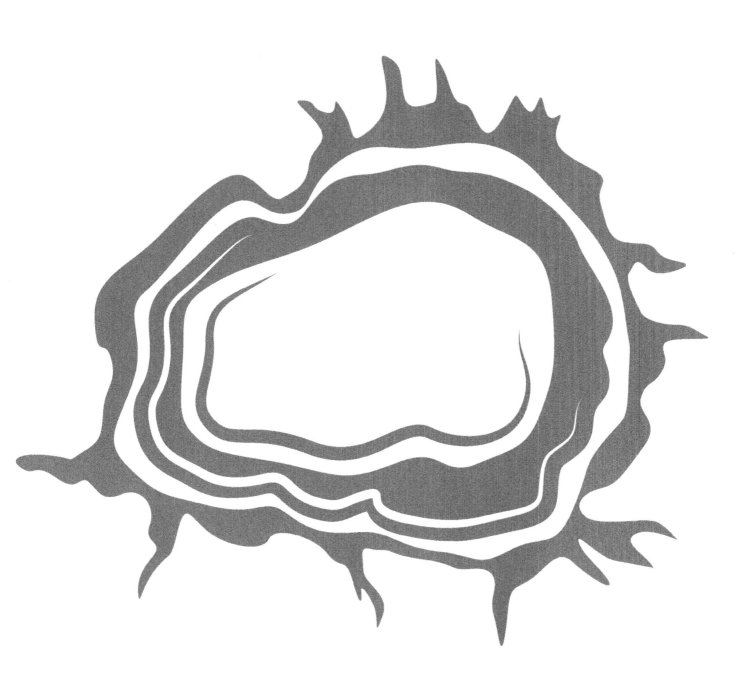

Would You Rather?

Ask your family these silly would you rather questions. Have each person explain why they picked that answer.

- ❏ Would you rather hike five miles backward or watch Old Faithful erupt 20 times?
- ❏ Would you rather smell the volcanic sulfur or the inside of your shoes?
- ❏ Would you rather go to Yellowstone or the Grand Tetons?
- ❏ Would you rather swim in an icy river in January or hike in 100 degrees?
- ❏ Would you rather lay on the beach or climb a mountain?
- ❏ Would you rather see a grizzly bear or a coyote?
- ❏ Would you rather run as fast as a deer or be as strong as a bison?
- ❏ Would you rather fly like a bald eagle or live in the mountains like a big horned sheep?
- ❏ Would you rather follow the tracks of a red fox or find a bird's nest?
- ❏ Would you rather be awake in the daytime or be nocturnal like an owl?
- ❏ Would you rather be as tall as a lodgepole pine or be small like a marmot?
- ❏ Would you rather explore an unknown area of the park or stick to the trails?
- ❏ Would you rather hike or snowshoe through Yellowstone Park?
- ❏ Would you rather find a beautiful flower or dig in the dirt for a colored rock?
- ❏ Would you rather walk by a lake or on a mountain trail?

HOW DO THEY PREDICT OLD FAITHFUL?

Old Faithful is a fairly predictable geyser. Ever want to know how the Park Rangers predict when Old Faithful will erupt? Below is the formula that they use to predict when the geyser will erupt.

You'll need to know when Old Faithful erupted last to do this. Check out the Live Old Faithful webcam to try this at home before you go on your trip. Or test this out when you get to Yellowstone.

https://www.nps.gov/yell/learn/photosmultimedia/webcams.htm

A.   Start Time _____

B.   End Time_____

C.   Length of Eruption (to the nearest ½ minute)_____

Look at C (Length of Eruption). Was it less than 3 minutes or more than 3 minutes?

Less than 3 minutes ⟶ 68 minutes

More than 3 minutes ⟶ 94 minutes

My prediction time = _____ + _____ = _____
                            (Start Time)   (68 min or 94 min)

Check your prediction on the webcam or in person. How close was your prediction?

Have You Seen Me?

The Yellowstone and Grand Teton area is known for a wide variety of wildlife. According to the National Park Services Statistics, there are over 400 species of wildlife from amphibians to eagles and bison. With so many interesting animals from large to small, see how many you can find. Check them off as you find them.

Bison

WHEN?

WHERE?

HOW MANY?

Bighorn Sheep

WHEN?

WHERE?

HOW MANY?

Elk

WHEN?

WHERE?

HOW MANY?

Moose

WHEN?

WHERE?

HOW MANY?

Photos provided by NPS

Have You Seen Me?

Mountain Goat

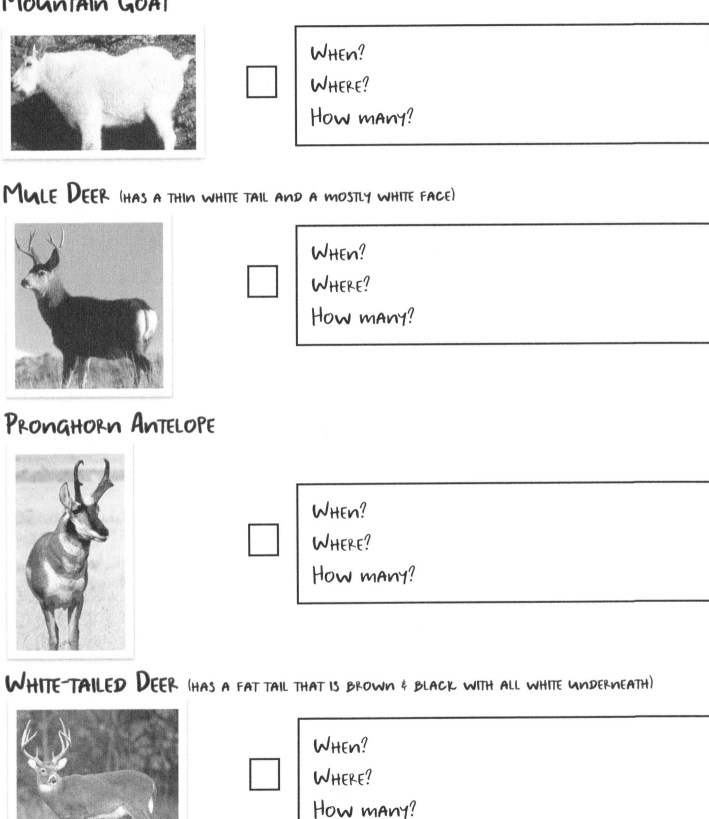

☐ When?
When?
Where?
How many?

Mule Deer (HAS A THIN WHITE TAIL AND A MOSTLY WHITE FACE)

☐ When?
Where?
How many?

Pronghorn Antelope

☐ When?
Where?
How many?

White-Tailed Deer (HAS A FAT TAIL THAT IS BROWN & BLACK WITH ALL WHITE UNDERNEATH)

☐ When?
Where?
How many?

Photos provided by NPS

Have You Seen Me?

Black Bear (no back hump, tall pointed ears, & shorter claws)

☐

When?

Where?

How many?

Grizzly Bear (have a back hump, short round ears, & longer claws)

☐

When?

Where?

How many?

Cougar or Mountain Lion

☐

When?

Where?

How many?

Coyote

☐

When?

Where?

How many?

Photos provided by NPS

Have You Seen Me?

Gray Wolf

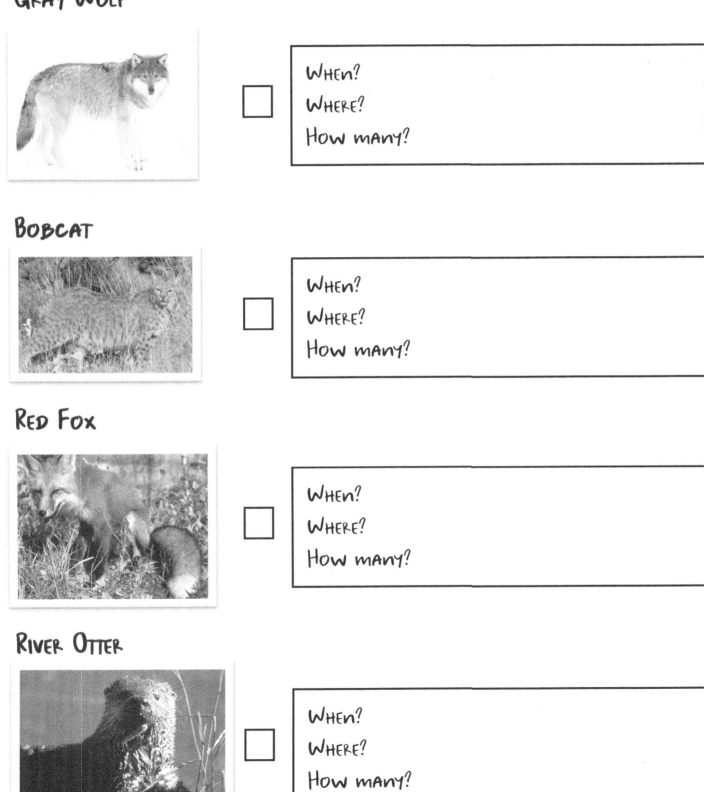

☐ When?
When?
Where?
How many?

Bobcat

☐ When?
Where?
How many?

Red Fox

☐ When?
Where?
How many?

River Otter

☐ When?
Where?
How many?

Photos provided by NPS

Have You Seen Me?

Beaver

☐

When?

Where?

How many?

Golden-mantled Ground Squirrel

☐

When?

Where?

How many?

Chipmunk

☐

When?

Where?

How many?

Red Squirrel

☐

When?

Where?

How many?

Photos provided by NPS

Have You Seen Me?

Yellow-bellied Marmot

When?

Where?

How many?

White-tailed Jackrabbit

When?

Where?

How many?

Skunk

When?

Where?

How many?

Bat

When?

Where?

How many?

Photos provided by NPS

Have You Seen Me?

Chickadee

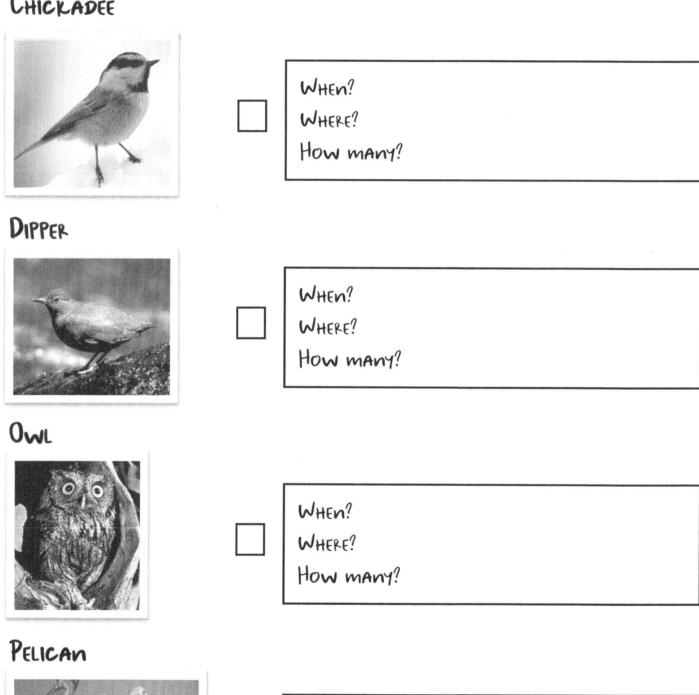

When?
Where?
How many?

Dipper

When?
Where?
How many?

Owl

When?
Where?
How many?

Pelican

When?
Where?
How many?

Photos provided by NPS

WHAT'S YOUR FAVORITE WILDLIFE?

Draw a picture of your favorite animal you have seen during your trip! Or paste in a picture you took of that animal.

CHALLENGE QUESTION

are we there Yet?

COOLEST OR MOST INTERESTING ROAD SIGN? TAKE A PICTURE BY IT IF YOU CAN.

CHALLENGE QUESTION

are we
there
Yet?

The Funniest thing that happened on your trip

CHALLENGE QUESTION

are we there Yet?

The state licence plate you saw that was furthest from your home. Who saw it? What do you know about that state and would you ever want to go there?

CHALLENGE QUESTION

are we there yet?

YOUR FAVORITE MOMENT OF THE WHOLE TRIP

CHALLENGE QUESTION

What new fact did you learn? Bonus points for taking a picture of the plaque or sign with the information on it!

CHALLENGE QUESTION

THE MOST SURPRISING THING THAT HAPPENED ON YOUR TRIP

CHALLENGE QUESTION

are we
there
yet?

The best, most interesting, or worst place you ate. Why? What did you eat (or not eat)?

CHALLENGE QUESTION

are we there Yet?

WHAT WAS YOUR FAVORITE ANIMAL YOU SAW? BONUS POINTS FOR TAKING A PICTURE OF IT.

NOTES

NOTES

NOTES

NOTES

NOTES

NOTES

NOTES

NOTES

NOTES

NOTES

NOTES

Notes

Answer Key

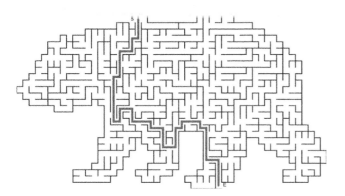

Page 47

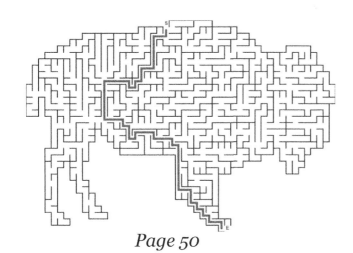

Page 50

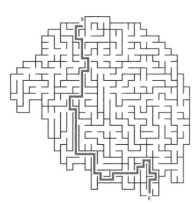

Page 55

		P											
M			E										
O			L										
U		C		I									
N			H	B		C							
T				I			A						
A				S	C			N					
I				O		K							
N				N	R		A		D				
			E	L	G	A	E	D					
			D	I	P	P	E	R	E				
							L	B	R	E			
							K						
	E	N	O	T	S	W	O	L	L	E	Y		

Page 46

OCOEYT	=	COYOTE
RATOMM	=	MARMOT
YOERSP	=	OSPREY
AIPMSICRT	=	PRISMATIC
LITAR	=	TRAIL
RTCKSA	=	TRACKS
SNBIO	=	BISON
LGIZYZR	=	GRIZZLY
EHIK	=	HIKE

Page 48

Answer Key

Page 51

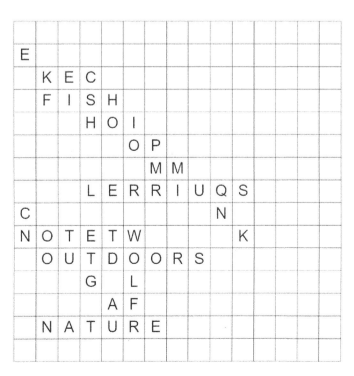

Page 56

Made in the USA
Coppell, TX
10 July 2025

51647543R00050